W9-AEY-118

Dear Parents:

Congratulations! Your child is taking the first steps on an exciting journey. The destination? Independent reading!

STEP INTO READING® will help your child get there. The program offers five steps to reading success. Each step includes fun stories and colorful art or photographs. In addition to original fiction and books with favorite characters, there are Step into Reading Non-Fiction Readers, Phonics Readers and Boxed Sets, Sticker Readers, and Comic Readers—a complete literacy program with something to interest every child.

Learning to Read, Step by Step!

Ready to Read   Preschool–Kindergarten
• big type and easy words • rhyme and rhythm • picture clues
For children who know the alphabet and are eager to begin reading.

Reading with Help   Preschool–Grade 1
• basic vocabulary • short sentences • simple stories
For children who recognize familiar words and sound out new words with help.

Reading on Your Own   Grades 1–3
• engaging characters • easy-to-follow plots • popular topics
For children who are ready to read on their own.

Reading Paragraphs   Grades 2–3
• challenging vocabulary • short paragraphs • exciting stories
For newly independent readers who read simple sentences with confidence.

Ready for Chapters   Grades 2–4
• chapters • longer paragraphs • full-color art
For children who want to take the plunge into chapter books but still like colorful pictures.

STEP INTO READING® is designed to give every child a successful reading experience. The grade levels are only guides; children will progress through the steps at their own speed, developing confidence in their reading.

Remember, a lifetime love of reading starts with a single step!

Published in the United States by Random House Children's Books, a division of Penguin Random House LLC, 1745 Broadway, New York, NY 10019, and in Canada by Penguin Random House Canada Limited, Toronto.

Step into Reading, Random House, and the Random House colophon are registered trademarks of Penguin Random House LLC.

Visit us on the Web!
StepIntoReading.com
rhcbooks.com

Educators and librarians, for a variety of teaching tools, visit us at RHTeachersLibrarians.com

ISBN 978-0-593-42527-5 (trade) — ISBN 978-0-593-42528-2 (lib. bdg.)

Printed in the United States of America

10 9 8 7 6 5 4 3 2 1

by Christy Webster

based on the teleplay by
Christopher Kennan and Kate Splaine

illustrated by Fernando Güell

Random House 🏠 New York

It is summer.

Barbie is excited to attend

an Arts Academy in New York.

She has traveled from Malibu

to study singing, dancing, and acting.

Barbie moves into her new room.

Her roommate is named Barbie, too!

This Barbie is from Brooklyn.

They call each other

Brooklyn and Malibu.

They go to class together.
The dean tells them one student
will sing a spotlight solo!

In dance class,

the two Barbies dance.

Brooklyn is very good!

Malibu learns to stage fight.

She learns music.

She is nervous.

Malibu does not do well.

Pop star Emmie is attending
their school, too.
She wants to make friends.
She wants to sing better.

Her father just wants her

to sing the spotlight solo.

Everyone is at practice.

Malibu stumbles.

She bumps into Brooklyn.

Brooklyn falls.

Malibu feels bad.

But Brooklyn will be better soon.

The dean thinks Malibu

pushed Brooklyn!

She tells Malibu to leave.

Brooklyn finds a video.

She shows it to the dean.

Malibu did not push Brooklyn.

Emmie's dad was afraid

Brooklyn would get the solo.

He lied to get

Emmie the spotlight solo.

Brooklyn goes to find Malibu.

Brooklyn tells Malibu

she can come back.

Malibu can't wait!

The friends are happy
to be back together.

Malibu works hard.

She enjoys herself.

She gets better in her classes.

At the end of the summer,

the dean chooses the soloist.

It is Barbie—both Barbies!

They sing and dance together.

Everything is better

with friends!